Ellie May

on April Fools' Day

WHOOPIE CUSHION

Ellie May

on April Fools' Day

Hillary Homzie

illustrated by Jeffrey Ebbeler

Charlesbridge

Published by Charlesbridge
85 Main Street
Watertown, MA 02472
(617) 926-0329
www.charlesbridge.com

Library of Congress Cataloging-in-Publication Data
Names: Homzie, Hillary, author. | Ebbeler, Jeffrey, illustrator.
Title: Ellie May on April Fools' Day / Hillary Homzie; illustrated by Jeffrey Ebbeler.
Description: Watertown, MA: Charlesbridge, [2018] | Summary: Ellie May really wants to be funnier than the class clown on April Fools' Day, however her enthusiasm turns the day into a bit of a disaster—but maybe remembering the best kind of humor and her own strengths can turn things around.
Identifiers: LCCN 2017043611 (print) | LCCN 2017059485 (ebook) | ISBN 9781632896773 (ebook) | ISBN 9781632896780 (ebook pdf) | ISBN 9781580898201 (reinforced for library use) | ISBN 9781580899291 (pbk.)
Subjects: LCSH: April Fools' Day—Juvenile fiction. | Practical jokes—Juvenile fiction. | Best friends—Juvenile fiction. | Self-control—Juvenile fiction. | Families—Juvenile fiction. |
Elementary schools—Juvenile fiction. | CYAC: April Fools' Day—Fiction. | Practical jokes—Fiction. | Best friends—Fiction. | Friendship—Fiction. | Self-control—Fiction. | Family life—Fiction. | Schools—Fiction.
Classification: LCC PZ7.H7458 (ebook) | LCC PZ7.H7458 Ei 2018 (print) | DDC 813.54—dc23
LC record available at https://lccn.loc.gov/2017043611

Printed in China
(hc) 10 9 8 7 6 5 4 3 2 1
(sc) 10 9 8 7 6 5 4 3 2 1

Illustrations done in black acrylic paint on hot press Fabriano paper and shaded digitally
Display type set in Canvas by Yellow Design Studio
Text type set in Calisto MT by Monotype Corporation
Printed by 1010 Printing International Limited in Huizhou, Guangdong, China
Production supervision by Brian G. Walker
Designed by Diane M. Earley

To Adia and Katie, elementary school students who each hold a Master's in practical jokes and a PhD in laughter—H. H.

For Isabel—J. E.

Chapter One

The Funniest

"Guess what's happening?" Ava said during morning sharing. She stood next to Ms. Silva, in front of the class.

"What!?" I shouted.

"Let's give Ava our best listening ears, Ellie May," Ms. Silva told me.

"It's really special, and it's marked here." Ava pointed to the calendar.

To see better, I scooted forward, careful to

stay on the rug. I like to pretend the tile floor is a gross swamp that I can't go near. But Max pushed me off the edge of the rug, so of course I elbowed him back.

"Keep your hands to yourself, Ellie May," said Ms. Silva.

"I'm just trying to stay away from the alligators that live on that part of the floor," I explained.

Everyone looked confused until Mo stretched his arms out in front of him and clapped them together like big jaws.

"Chomp, chomp," he bellowed.

Lots of kids laughed like it was the funniest thing in the entire universe.

"It's time for everyone to put your hands in your laps," said Ms. Silva. "Lock them and freeze them." She demonstrated.

I put my hands in my lap, clasped my hands

together, and tried to think about them being frozen like ice cubes or popsicles.

Still standing in front of the class, Ava sighed. She likes to pretend she's a grown-up.

"Let's give Ava our attention again, class," said Ms. Silva.

"Monday will be extra, *extra* special." Ava jutted her chin so high it looked like her neck grew five inches. "I'll be celebrating my birthday at school. My real birthday is Sunday, March 31. My parents are taking me to the theater." She said it *theater* all fancy. "But on Monday, I'm bringing in allergen-free cupcakes for the class. They'll be *homemade*. Mom and I make them from scratch, using organic ingredients."

The class wiggled their fingers in the air to give Ava a big ten-finger woo. But my shoulders got slumpy. Slumpy is how I feel when my science-fair volcano doesn't have the biggest eruption. Or when I'm not called on to be flag leader for the Pledge of Allegiance.

My birthday was last month. I had wanted to bring in cupcakes too, but Mom and Dad got their wires mixed up, or whatever they say happens when they both forget very important things like birthday cupcakes. So I brought in a box of animal crackers instead. No one cares about *animal crackers*.

"This Monday is going to be *so* yummy," said Pablo, rubbing his belly.

"Hey, Monday is also April Fools' Day!" Mo called out. "Monday should get a new name. *Monday Funday*!" Tilting his head, he stuck out his tongue and pulled on his lips. All the kids laughed really hard. I wish I had thought to say, "Monday Funday."

Beside me, Lizzy whispered, "Mo's so funny." Even my very best friend can't get enough of Mo.

Max made a goofy face right along with Mo. He's a professional copycat.

Ms. Silva gave us her Teacher Look, where she squints until her eyelids almost touch. "Yes, it's April Fools' Day. But remember that anyone who wants to celebrate needs to do it in good fun, or not at all. You don't want to scare or hurt anyone. My mother once pulled a good-natured prank on our family. She cooked scoops of mashed potatoes with black beans in them. When we opened the oven, my siblings and I thought she'd made us chocolate chip cookies!"

I never would've guessed Ms. Silva had a mom *that* funny.

"*So*, Ms. Silva," said Mo, "that means on April Fools' Day we can give someone a funny meal, but we can't toss mealy worms on them?"

Nearly everyone cracked up. Even Ms. Silva smiled as she nodded. Ava smiled a bit, but she didn't laugh. She was serious about sharing her birthday plan.

Maybe I could be as funny as Mo. Maybe I could be the funniest. I could make April Fools' Day a holiday the whole class would remember.

Normally Monday isn't my favorite day of the week. Mondays are the opposite of Saturdays, when my family plays a game or watches a movie. Everyone has fun. But on Mondays there are grumpy faces scrambling to finish homework, to get to school or work, and to walk Diesel without forgetting to pick up his doggy doo-doo.

This Monday was going to be *waaaaay* different.

Chapter Two

Giddyup

At recess Lizzy was playing foursquare. Tons of kids waited in line.

"C'mon," I called. "Let's go to the monkey bars."

Lizzy thumped the red ball into Mo's square. He slammed it into another square.

"I'm not out yet," Lizzy said. This was a surprise, considering how she normally plays.

"Okay, I'll cheer for you." I raised my hands

in the air, pretending to wave swishy pom-poms. "Way to go, Lizzy!"

Owen smashed the ball into Lizzy's square. She missed the return by a hair.

"Out!" yelled Pablo.

Lizzy pushed up her glasses and harrumphed. "I never win." She looked slumpy.

"It's okay. You'll win next time." I grabbed her hand, and we zigzagged around a kickball game on the playing field. A wind blew, and the long grass tickled our ankles.

"Want to spin in circles and fall down in dizziness?"

"Not really." Lizzy studied clumps of plants by the fence. "How about looking for daisies and making chains. Or drawing together?"

"Too much sitting around."

Lizzy let out a long breath. She likes not-moving-around-too-much games. I like bouncy games. I was itching to move and talk at the same time. "C'mon, let's go to the monkey bars." I tugged her forward.

"I guess so," she said.

"We'll be the blister sisters!" I raced to the monkey bars, and Lizzy chugged behind me.

I scrambled up the ladder. "It's going to be a happy time soon! Because Monday is April Fools' Day, and I am going to do a prank that will get everyone laughing the most."

Just as I said that, Mo and Max thudded past us to the swings. Lizzy smiled at them, and I could see her missing front tooth. "Like Mo?"

"Even funnier than Mo," I told her.

"Why do you care so much about April Fools' Day anyway?"

"Lizzy. It is our *job* to worry about being funny on April Fools' Day. When it's Thanksgiving you should be thankful and eat lots of pumpkin pie with whipped cream. On Halloween you're supposed to put on a costume and not worry about cavities. And on April Fools' Day it's a total waste if you don't do goofy stuff like put Vaseline on doorknobs."

"I guess you have a point," she said.

"Hurry!" I cried out. "On the ground there's a giant octopus with suction cups."

"That slurps up people?" Lizzy asked. Her aquamarine glasses fogged, and she looked cool and mysterious. "I'm coming!" She scurried up the ladder and swung toward the center of the monkey bars. From the other side I shimmied to the center. We hung there together, dangling our legs. On the playing field, kids cheered because someone scored. It felt like they were cheering for us.

"Phew," said Lizzy. "That was close. Look down below. Giant squids that squirt poison are coming!" I scooted backward to let Lizzy swing across to my side.

That was when the horse group came trotting up to the monkey bars. The queen of the horses is Jamila. She swished her long hair and clomped her feet. The rest of the girls followed close behind. They pranced and neighed. Normally Ava reads a giant book with lots of chapters during recess. But today she was trotting right along.

"Ava, you make a speedy horse," I called out. She neighed. Jamila and the other three horses neighed too.

"I'm taking horseback-riding lessons after school," said Ava with a whinny. "It's an early birthday present from my grandparents." She reared up and tossed back her mane.

"Well, you better gallop away. There's a poisonous squid next to you," I explained with a grin. "Your hoof's going to get sprayed with squid ink!"

I waited for the laughter. Only nobody was

looking at me. Instead they were all looking at Mo, who stumbled up to the monkey bars like his legs were made of Jell-O. "The mud's so slippery," he moaned. "I can't lift my giant horse legs." Max raced up next to him.

Mo wobbled helplessly on one leg and began to purposely flop to the ground. "Help, I'm falling!" he yelled. "And I can't *giddyap*!"

Everyone laughed super hard. The horse girls giggled and pawed at the ground before Mo and Max raced over to the swings.

Mo was so lucky. He made every day as funny as April Fools' Day.

I let out a long sigh.

"Did you say something?" asked Lizzy.

"Only inside my head," I admitted.

Chapter Three

An Antsy Idea

After school Dad said I could go on the computer to read about April Fools' Day. The holiday started hundreds of years ago. People all over the world celebrate it in different ways. In France they put paper fish on people's backs. Thankfully they don't use the stinky real fish Dad likes to bake. In India they have a spring festival called Holi where you are supposed to laugh and throw colored powder. In Scotland they like April Fools' so much they celebrate it for two whole days.

I had to figure out the best way I could celebrate and be the funniest. I began to look for silly inspiration in my big sister's room. Maybe I could find something messy like the colorful powder in India. Tiptoeing upstairs, I read the sign on Lexie's door: *Keep Out! Private Property!* Do all twelve-year-olds put up bossy signs like that? I listened to see if anyone was coming and then snuck inside.

Wagging his tail, Diesel bounded into the bedroom after me. He's a labradoodle, which means he has curly brown hair just like me. I put my fingers to my lips, which was a big mistake because Diesel thought I had food for him. His swishy tail almost knocked down Lexie's alarm clock.

That gave me an April Fools' Day idea.

I could make the clocks at school say the wrong time. That way, as soon as we got to school, it'd be time to leave! Everyone would love it.

I scooped up Lexie's clock and grinned. Too bad I didn't know how to set the time. Why does a hand on the six mean thirty minutes, anyway? Forget this trick.

Next I tiptoed into my parents' bedroom. Mom has a trillion pairs of shoes. Maybe I could put something crazy in someone's shoes at school. Like a bug. But I'd have to catch one first. And what if I couldn't find any of the good wiggly or slimy kind of bugs? Or what if Ms. Silva thought this was too scary or hurtful? I couldn't risk it.

Finally I crept down to the kitchen. I didn't want Lexie to hear. Our family room and kitchen are one big place. Only you sit on the couch in the family room. And you watch Mom and Dad cook in the kitchen.

Lexie sat in the family room, reading to Midge. That's because Midge is three and can't read yet. She just memorizes her favorite books and pretends to read.

I started poking around the kitchen. Maybe I could find one of Dad's stinky fish in there. Diesel was still on my trail. I scratched him behind his ears, and his tail wagged even harder. I looked over at the glass jars labeled *flour*, *sugar*, and *tea*.

Hey, I could put salt in the sugar jar!

At a sleepover at Lizzy's, I once had the idea to put salt in her dad's coffee. It really worked, because he spit it right out. I could give kids salt instead of sugar. That would make everyone laugh. Hmmm. If only kids at my school drank coffee. This idea wouldn't work.

I was hungry, so I grabbed a box of squishy raisins. I like raisins because they are sweet like candy but nobody tells you to stop eating them.

I stared at the raisin between my fingers and squeezed it. Hey, wait a minute. The raisin looked just like something else.

Something that crawls on things.

An ant!

When I was little, a hundred million years ago, in first grade, when I couldn't sit still, my nana would say, "Do you have ants in your pants, Ellie May?" and everyone in my family would laugh.

Ants are definitely funny. Even grown-ups think so.

I could definitely pretend the raisin was an ant.

I scooped up a napkin. Only I did it so fast that the napkin holder dropped onto the floor with a *ka-thud*!

"What are you doing?" called Lexie from the family room.

"Cleaning," I said, waving a paper napkin.

"You spilled!" said Midge. She pointed with Betty, her stuffed giraffe.

At the sound of the word *spill*, Diesel bounded over. His most favorite words are *spill* and *treat*.

Diesel sniffed at the floor with big, sad brown

eyes. He had expected a good spill. The food kind. So I opened the fridge and searched for something he might like for me to accidentally drop, as part of my ant joke. Cheese slices? Nope. Brussels sprouts? Yuck! Mustard? Nah.

Above the little pullout drawer, I discovered a jar of natural peanut butter. Yes! It's what we use when we spread peanut butter on celery and top that with raisins to look like ants on a log.

Diesel sniffed and snuffed and watched me purposefully drop the jar at his feet.

Kerplunk! The peanut butter jar crashed onto the floor.

"Oh, drat! I dropped it!"

"What was that?" asked Midge.

"Nothing," I said. The jar didn't have a top because the lid had mysteriously disappeared. So the foil cover flew off, and blobs of peanut butter oil oozed onto the floor.

Diesel slurped up the spill with his big pink tongue, faster than ever.

"Hey!" Lexie jumped up from the couch. "Don't let the dog eat that." Midge followed her over. "Will you stop dropping stuff in here?"

"Don't worry—it wasn't a whole lot of peanut butter," I explained. "See, there was an ant crawling over the floor, but I got it by throwing the peanut butter jar at it." I waved my napkin quickly so the raisin would look like a blurry ant inside the paper. "Look! A dead ant."

"Gross!" Lexie declared.

"Yeah, I'm an ant killer *and* I'm an ant eater." I popped the raisin into my mouth, chewed, and patted my stomach.

"What is wrong with you?" yelled Lexie.

Midge's eyes got as big as beetles. She started to giggle. "What do ants taste like?"

"Spicy," I explained. "Mmmm. So good!"

"Yuck!" Lexie made a lemon face. But she was also smirking.

Mom flew out of her home office at the same time as Dad hurried into the kitchen. He was carrying boxes full of giant food, so I knew he had been shopping at one of those supersized stores.

"What's going on?" Dad asked.

Mom studied Diesel licking the floor and the peanut butter jar. She studied the napkin crumpled in my hand.

Lexie slapped her hands on her hips. "Ellie May let the dog eat peanut butter."

"And she ate an ant!" Midge giggled.

Dad set the groceries on the counter. "Can someone please explain?"

"It's homework," I said.

"How is that"—Lexie pointed to the now clean floor—"homework?"

"Well, April Fools' is on Monday, so I want to

be funny at school. Right now I'm working on a joke plan at home, so it's *home*work."

"Now it all makes sense," said Dad. I guess since he works from home as a writer, he understands the definition of homework. After all, he does it every day!

Mom smiled like she was remembering something. "One April Fools' I kidnapped Uncle Matt's stuffed walrus and left a ransom note asking for chocolate bars before I'd give it back." She grabbed some cartons of almond milk from the box of groceries and stuffed them in the fridge. "I got in big trouble for that one."

"That's kind of mean, Mom." Wow. I couldn't believe my own grown-up mother admitted she did something not so nice.

"It led to lots of hurt feelings." She rolled her eyes and winced.

Dad shoved some pasta sauce into a cabinet.

"Apparently Ellie May's funny bone is your fault, Beatrice." That's my mom's grown-up real name. Her nickname is Bea. It's a nice kind of insect name for people. If Jamila and Ava were bugs, they'd be called horseflies. I should use that joke next recess!

Mom whirled around. "Hey, where did Midge go?"

Midge waved on the other side of the sliding glass door. "Here," she said, holding a stick with a bunch of ants crawling on it. "I'm an ant finder! I'm hungry!" She held out her giraffe. "So's Betty!"

"No!" we all called out.

My parents and Lexie had to explain to Midge that my ant wasn't actually a real ant.

"I think your April Fools' joke worked," Dad said, setting the table for dinner.

"A little too well," added Mom.

"It was pretty funny, Ellie May," admitted Lexie. "But you have to stop feeding Diesel people food."

"I'll remember," I said, trying really hard not to let her get my goat. This means not letting yourself get mad at someone. I don't know what goats have to do with it, though, since I've never met a goat before.

I was in too good a mood anyway. I was going to do the ant joke on April Fools' Day. It was perfect!

Chapter Four
Go Big or Go Home

During lunch on Friday, Ava and the horse bunch trotted toward Lizzy and me and sat down at a table by the salad bar. Normally they eat by the healthy food pyramid poster hanging over the dessert station.

The place was loud and packed with second and third graders. There was no Ms. Silva. Lunch is when she takes a vacation from all of us. Lunchroom monitors like Mrs. Rumsky buzzed about, commanding kids to "sit in your seat" and "be respectful."

"Hey, horsey girls!" I called out, hoping everyone nearby would hear. "Come over to the salad bar. And get some hay."

"There's no hay there," said Jamila.

"It's a lettuce bin," said Ava, sitting down with the herd. "It has romaine and spinach. Hay is golden colored."

"Well, sometimes the lettuce at school is yellow," I said, with a grin. Lizzy giggled. But no one else seemed to notice my joke.

Mrs. Rumsky didn't notice me either, thankfully. She does not like us to do fun stuff like yell jokes to each other, play trash-can basketball, or balance sporks on our noses. "I hope that on April Fools' Day Mrs. Rumsky isn't so strict and lets me be extra funny," I said.

"Mrs. Rumsky has eyes in the back of her head,"

said Lizzy. "What are you planning, anyway?"

"I'm planning to make April Fools' the most fun day ever, ever, *ever*."

"How?" Lizzy tore open her ketchup packet.

"By being the funniest kid in the class," I explained.

Lizzy spurted a glob of ketchup next to her fish sticks. Only she didn't make regular globs. She swirled her ketchup so they looked like lollipops. Even when she ate, Lizzy made masterpieces.

"Maybe I'll use fake blood as a joke," I said. I wasn't ready to let her in on the ant surprise just yet.

"Ellie May, that could scare someone."

"But it would be ketchup."

"It *looks* like blood. Plus it stains. You could get in trouble."

"Oh," I said, feeling a little fizzled and flat.

"You're funny in your own way, Ellie May. Without fake blood," Lizzy added.

Suddenly a balled-up napkin whooshed past my chin and bopped Lizzy right on the nose. Another balled-up napkin landed on my sandwich. The cafeteria monitor was nowhere in sight.

"Got you!" hollered Max.

Lizzy turned as red as her packet of ketchup and laughed along with everyone at Mo's table.

When nobody was looking, I tossed my balled-up napkin toward Max.

I missed.

"Nice try, Ellie May," Lizzy said.

That's when I decide it was time to show Lizzy my ant joke. As my grandpa always says, "You have to go big or go home." I whipped out my box of raisins and explained how on April Fools' I was going to pretend a single little raisin was an ant and eat it.

Lizzy blinked. "I don't understand. Ants don't look like raisins. I've drawn ants a lot. Especially ants at a picnic. They have six legs. Raisins don't have legs."

"It's small, though. And I'll move it. It'll look . . ."

"Smudgy?" asked Lizzy. "From a distance?"

She squinted at the raisin pinched between my fingers.

"Yes! See!" I flicked the raisin onto the floor, waited a second, then scooped it up and ate it. "Oh, yum!" I said. "An ant for dessert!"

Only Mrs. Rumsky stomped right up to me at that same moment. She waved her arms. She blew her whistle. "No eating insects in the cafeteria!" she shouted in a voice louder than a megaphone.

The horse girls' jaws dropped. Their mouths were so big you could fit a whole box of raisins inside. Kids were pointing and whispering. No one was really laughing.

"No," I said, protesting. "It was actually a raisin, I was just—"

Mrs. Rumsky stared at the balled-up napkins on the table. "And clean up that mess."

"Okay," I said cheerfully and held up my box of raisins. "I will be sure to throw away this box of raisins as well. Since it's definitely dried fruit and not full of ants. I fooled you all."

No one was paying attention anymore.

Lizzy giggled. "Ellie May, you're the silliest."

Yeah, the silliest for no longer having a perfect ant joke for April Fools' Day.

Chapter Five

One Sneaky Bird

After lunch we had to learn about bird stuff. Only I knew it wouldn't be anything useful, like how to lay an egg. Or how to fly to school.

"I think you'll find some really unique and interesting facts," said Ms. Silva, handing everybody bird books. "To find things, remember to use the subheadings."

"And the indexes," added Ava.

"Exactly." Ms. Silva smiled. "Class, please read silently. Then you'll have time to talk with your desk partner about the fascinating bird facts you've found."

My desk partner was Pablo. Talking about birds with him would be fun. We both opened our books and got to it.

"Wow. There must be a gazillion bird facts in this thing. This book is really thick," I moaned.

Pablo chuckled.

"Not for me," Mo said. He spread his arms out superwide. "*This* is a thick book for me!"

Pablo chuckled even harder.

Figures. Everything seems to be so much funnier with Mo in the mix.

I turned to my book. At first I couldn't find neat bird stuff, but then I started reading about some really cool birds.

I made a list of my favorite discoveries.

1) Many birds, like cardinals, take an ant bath. They cover their feathers with ants. The ants let out acid that can kill fungus. Some people think this might make ants taste better before the birds eat them. (I better not tell Midge about this!)

2) Homing pigeons were used to carry messages over long distances. They never got lost. During ancient times they flew to villages in Greece to announce the winners of the Olympics.

3) Bearded vultures are really into style. They dye their white feathers by rubbing themselves in red dirt. It's supposed to make them look fancy.

4) The rock wren builds a patio outside its nest. Sometimes the bird uses 300 stones! (We need a new patio. Mom should call a wren.)

5) Sociable weavers live in bird apartment buildings. They're crowded. Up to 400–500 birds live in these giant nests, which look like huge haystacks stuck in trees.

6) Scrub jays hide their acorn food for the winter. If they see another animal spying on them while they're storing away their food, scrub jays play a trick. They bury stones instead of acorns. (How sneaky!)

When it was time to talk with our partners, Pablo told me all about ravens. “They can copy noises really well,” he said. “They can even sound like a minivan or a toilet.”

“Whoa! I bet people sometimes think their car is stuck up in a tree!”

Pablo lifted up his head, pretending to search up a tree, and we laughed.

I told Pablo all about the scrub jays and how they were super-duper tricky.

“I bet the squirrels and other animals are pretty surprised when they try to dig up the scrub jay’s food,” he said, “and they find stones instead.”

That got me thinking.

A scrub jay was the perfect April Fools’ Day bird.

Hmmm. What if I could be as tricky as this bird?

Chapter Six

Just Looking for a Snack

At the end of the day, a super sneaky, scrub jay April Fools' plan came to me. I'd give someone a beautifully wrapped present. They'd think it was something really nice and special. Kind of like other birds think they're going to find the scrub jay's buried acorns. But instead of a gift, I'd wrap up ugly old vegetables! Everyone would be so surprised and laugh so hard. Maybe I could use a turnip, because they taste like dirt. Or spinach.

That stuff is as slimy as seaweed and sticks in your teeth. I know because last time we were at Huntington City Beach I tried some seaweed and had to spit it right out on the sand. *Blech!*

I had the extra-perfect plan for April Fools' Day, and now I couldn't wait to get home. Only the end of school took ten hundred years because we had to copy spelling words. Some of them were regular, like *desk* and *always*. And one was the tricky bonus word *listen*, with a super sneaky and silent *t*. That word was trying to trick people.

But then again, so was I!

Right after school I zoomed past my sisters in the family room and zipped to the kitchen to find some yucky vegetables. I flung open the fridge door.

Lexie jumped up from where she was doing homework. "Are you up to something again?" she said in her bossiest voice.

"Just looking for a snack." A nice blast of freezy air made my face feel super good. I could see clear back to the dill-pickle jars and sauerkraut.

Midge popped up and raced over. "I want a snack too."

Lexie closed her three-ring binder. "I'll get it for you. Ellie May, what are you looking for?"

"I don't know," I lied. "But I need a whole bunch of it."

Lexie hustled over to me. "You can't find something if you don't know what you're looking for."

"Vegetables," I admitted.

That's when Lexie hugged her middle, laughing. Her whole face looked as purple as the eggplant in the fridge. "Ha, ha, ha," she said. "That's a good one. Since when do *you* like vegetables?"

Midge started laughing too. She stood next to me. "Why am I laughing?" she asked.

"Vegetables," said Lexie. "Ellie May hates them." She opened a bin in the bottom of the fridge. "Here are some carrots and stuff."

I clapped my hands as I stared at all of those vegetables. "Perfect-o."

Lexie shrugged. "You better ask Dad first. He might want to use them for dinner." She strolled back to the family room and opened her binder. "This is a weird day."

Okay, so it was weird because of me. But weird is a good thing for funny people. Like clowns. They put red balls on their noses and wear shoes that are the wrong size.

I felt deep down in my bones that I was on the right path! I picked three perfect vegetables. A turnip, a brussels sprout—which is like a stinky, teeny cabbage—and a wedge of zucchini, full of icky seeds. I would've asked for permission before I took them, but Mom was at work, and Dad was on a writing deadline for one of his articles. You can't disturb him unless it's a big emergency. So I decided to write a letter:

Dear Mom and Dad,

If you see missing vegetables, don't get scared. A vegitarian robber didn't take them. It was me. Your own kid.

I only took the yucky ones. I need them to make the craziest, best, most exciting prank ever. It is so I can be funny for a funny holiday. It is called April Fools. You know about it. But maybe you forgot. I know you are bizy.

This is my permishun note.

Love,
Ellie May

Chapter Seven

My Life Is Saved!

While my vegetables were busy being vegetables that I would later wrap all fancy like real presents, I spent Saturday practicing other funny stuff to try out. If I was going to be the funniest on April Fools' Day—as funny as Mo—I needed a lot of material up my sleeve.

First I sprang out of a closet and scared Lexie. Only she didn't think it was funny. With a *kerplunk*, she dropped her binder. Papers whooshed through the air and covered the floor like giant snowflakes.

I had to apologize a million hundred times. Mom and Dad told me I couldn't pop out at people, but they didn't say I couldn't do it to *dogs*. So I jumped out at Diesel and played hide-and-seek. He loved it.

Too bad there aren't any labradoodles in my class.

Next I taped down the light switches. But the tape was old and peeled right off when anyone flicked them on.

I put pieces of cotton in my mom's shoes. Only she just pulled the cotton out and didn't say anything.

So I figured surprise vegetables were the best and yuckiest way to go.

On Sunday I flung open the closet door in the guest room. That's where we keep stuff for presents.

There were rolls of birthday paper with images of cakes and candles. Plus paper with pink and blue teddy bears for babies, and all kinds of razzle-dazzle things like red ribbons and peach bows. Only I didn't see what I wanted—shiny, foil-colored paper to wrap up my April Fools' presents.

Suddenly I heard the *thump thump* of little-sister feet. I should have made a keep-out sign.

Midge burst into the room. "What are you doing, Ellie May?"

"Nothing." I banged the closet door shut with a *whomp*.

"Please, please tell me," begged Midge. "I'll never bug you ever again."

I peered up. "I was just studying the ceiling."

"Liar, liar, pants on fire." Midge pointed to the closet with her cute, pudgy four-year-old finger. "Something's in there!" Yanking open the closet door, she dived right in.

"Stop it, Midge!" I pulled on her, but it was like trying to yank Diesel away from a steak sandwich. She kicked through ribbons, bows, and boxes. She shook gift bags.

"They're empty!" she wailed.

"It's Mommy's gift closet," I explained. "For other people, not us."

"No fair!" Midge's mouth turned frowny. "Hey, that's Betty!" She grabbed a bright orange giraffe from the re-gift shelf. That's where Mom puts toys she doesn't like or we already have. She doesn't think we should have two of anything.

"Midge, put that back," said Lexie, whooshing into the guest room. "That's not Betty. It's a giraffe that looks like Betty." Her hair was still wet from swim practice, only it wasn't drippy. Lexie dropped her gym bag onto the floor. "You two shouldn't be in here."

Midge hugged the giraffe tighter. "Mine!"

Lexie grabbed the giraffe away from Midge, tossed it back onto the re-gift shelf, and banged the closet door shut. Midge tried to open the closet, only Lexie blocked her.

Midge yelled and kicked the closet so hard her shoes flew right off.

"You're going to get a time-out," Lexie warned in a voice that sounded just like Mom's important-lawyer voice. Mom works for a place that is trying to save the ocean from garbage. The ocean is big, so Mom has to be really loud.

Midge whacked the closet even harder. The door rattled and shook.

I raced out of the room, searched Midge's bed, and found the real Betty. "Here you go, Midge. See?"

Midge stared at Betty. The giraffe's neck was droopy, and the fur was not so orange. It was the real one. Her eyes grew big. "Betty!" she screamed and hugged the giraffe so tight that if it had been a real live one, it would have thrown up its giraffe lunch.

Lexie turned to me as Midge continued to hug the real Betty. “You shouldn’t be in here,” she said, trying to sound like Mom again.

“I’m looking for wrapping paper. For school,” I explained.

“For school?” Lexie’s brows lifted. She loves school. If she could, she’d marry it.

I opened up the closet. All the wrapping paper, ribbons, and bows had fallen out of the turned-over bins and baskets. It was a jumbled-up mess. Except it made me happy. All that kicking had shaken stuff. Some silvery wrapping paper had slid to the bottom of the pile and appeared before my very eyes.

“My life is saved!” I said, grabbing the shiny paper. “This is exactly what I was looking for. You found it, Midge.”

"I did?"

"Yes!" I hugged Midge. Midge hugged Betty. "Sandwich hug!" I yelled.

"Sandwich hug!" yelled Midge.

That's when Dad came tromping upstairs.

"What's all the ruckus?" he asked.

He stared at me. He stared at Midge. "Sandwich hug!" she cried.

"I have something to tell you, Daddy," said Midge. "Betty has a twin that lives in there." She pointed to the closet. "And gift bags don't have presents inside. And I saved Ellie May's life."

Lexie and I laughed. Not an April Fools' Day kind of laugh. More like the kind of laugh that makes you love how stinkin' cute your little sister can be. Sometimes.

It took me ten hundred hours to wrap up the yucky vegetables. Rather than one present, I made three shiny silver packages. A brussels sprout one,

a turnip one, and a zucchini one. Now I just needed to figure out who I was going to do my scrub jay trick on.

Maybe I could do it on Pablo? He'd think it was super funny. But he does sit next to me. I had to wonder if he'd overheard my April Fools' planning. If I did it to Max, he might not think it was as funny because Mo didn't do it. And Lizzy was out of the question, obviously. She already knew I was up to something.

Suddenly I remembered we were going to celebrate Ava's birthday on Monday. An amazing thought zoomed into my head. I could prank Ava! It was going to be sooooo funny. Everyone would laugh and talk about it all day long. And Ava would feel like her birthday and April Fools' Day were mashed up into one big, fun, awesome celebration.

Chapter Eight

Wrapped Up and Ready

When I boarded the bus for school on Monday, the clouds looked like turnips. That was a very good sign.

I plopped down in a seat next to Lizzy, told her my plan, and gave her a big thumbs-up. "I'm ready."

After a few minutes the bus squealed to a stop. A boy with bright orange hair got on the bus, but not Ava. "That was her bus stop," I said.

Lizzy peered out the window. "Maybe she rode to school on her horse."

I laughed. "Knowing Ava, she would make sure to get a horse license first."

"Are you sure Ava won't get mad? What if you get in trouble?"

"I'll be fine," I promised. "It's April Fools'."

When the bus dropped us off, I looked all around for Ava.

There! She was standing in the drop-off circle, along with ten hundred other kids. Ava was dressed up in a flowy dress with peach flowers and shiny white shoes. She looked all razzle-dazzle.

"Why weren't you on the bus?" I asked.

"Because it's my birthday, silly." Ava smoothed her dress, which didn't need to be smoothed.

"Happy birthday!" Lizzy said.

"Thank you," Ava responded. "My mom and I baked birthday treats."

"Where are the treats?" I asked. Lizzy gave me a worried look.

"We already dropped them off in the classroom." Ava waved to her mom in a green minivan in the drop-off circle. Her mom blew kisses and Ava caught them. Then the minivan pulled away. "Those are birthday kisses," she explained.

"Oh." I pulled out the presents from my backpack once I knew Mo and Max and the horse girls were close by too. Everyone needed to see the scrub jay work her magic!

"For me?!" Ava was surprised I would get her something. It wasn't like she was my best friend or anything. But we were classmates, after all.

The other horses stepped closer to see better.

Ava carefully pried off the shiny bow and delicately began to unwrap the brussels sprout.

I shifted back and forth, waiting.

And waiting and waiting.

"Just rip it open!" I begged.

Ava moved even slower. "At our house we save wrapping paper because it's good for the earth."

It might be good for the earth, but it wasn't good for my patience. I bounced on my feet. I bit my fingernails.

Finally Ava stared at what was inside. A green leafy ball of stink, that's what!

"A brussels sprout?" she asked.

"Yes." I tried not to giggle. Ava's eyes grew big. She didn't say anything else.

"There's more!" I told her. Why wasn't anyone laughing yet?

With a "Ta-da!" Ava finished unwrapping her presents. She studied all the vegetables.

"Betcha didn't know there'd be vegetables inside," I chuckled, elbowing Lizzy to laugh along.

"You remembered, Ellie May!"

"Remembered what?" I stopped bouncing.

"That I started horseback-riding classes. Annabelle adores vegetables!"

"Annabelle?" I was stumped.

"Annabelle's the horse I'm training with. She'll eat these right up. She loves vegetables! And so do I." Ava pinched the gross brussels sprout between her thumb and pointer finger. "This is exactly the food that Annabelle needs," she said in a very serious voice. "It's full of vitamins."

"Awesome," said Jamila. "We can help feed it to her." The other horse girls clapped.

What! My heart dropped.

This wasn't like an April Fools' prank one bit. Ava was supposed to feel tricked and laugh, not talk about vitamins. I was supposed to be the extra-funny one today. I just didn't get it.

"So you actually *like* the presents?" I fidgeted with the zipper on my coat.

"Oh yes." She shook her head. "Here I thought

you were going to do a prank on me. Instead you were nice!"

I pushed my zipper all the way to the top. It felt cold on my chin. "Yes, that's me. So nice."

Ava turned to prance down the hallway in her peach flowery dress, holding the shiny wrapping paper and her vegetables. The horse girls trotted after her.

Folding my arms, I grumbled all the way to class.

"Hey, Ellie May," Mo yelled after me. "*Knock, knock*."

"Who's there?" I replied.

"Lettuce."

"Lettuce who?"

"Lettuce get out of here before you start giving us all broccoli!" he called out.

Everyone laughed. Of course they did! But yesterday, when I had tried a lettuce joke in the cafeteria, it hadn't worked. At all.

Chapter Nine
Binocular Vision

"When are we having Ava's birthday treat?" Pablo asked during morning sharing.

"After reading time," said Ms. Silva.

"Cool!" shouted a bunch of kids. Ava looked super proud.

"I can't wait to eat cupcakes," said Pablo, licking his lips.

Cupcakes might be my favorite food, especially the icing. "Right now we're going to learn about a very important tool," said Ms. Silva. She pulled binoculars out of a bag. "Can anyone tell me what this is for?"

Jamila raised her hand. "My grandparents have a pair. You use them to look at birds."

"Or planes," said Owen.

"Or to spy on people," I said hopefully.

"Well, we're not going to use them for spying, Ellie May," said Ms. Silva. "I received a science grant, and guess what? We now have six pairs for the classroom!" She pointed to a bucket filled with red binoculars. "They're especially made for kids."

Everyone in class gave a ten-finger woo.

"We're going to use our binoculars to help find the lirpaloof. That's a rare bird. It only comes around once a year. Some of them have been spotted right near here. A neighbor reported seeing one on the roof of the school and by the playground."

Lizzy looked at me, and I looked at her.

"A famous bird flies near our school?" I asked.

"Oh yes," said Ms. Silva. "Everyone around the world knows about this bird. Right after recess we will go out and scout for the lirpaloof."

After pulling down the screen, Ms. Silva pushed a button on her remote control. "This is what the lirpaloof looks like." I stared at an image of a large bird. It had a mostly red head, with black feathers on top that looked like a mohawk.

"Hey," I said, "black is Lizzy's second-favorite color." She uses a fancy black pen in her sketch book. When she lets me borrow it, I turn into a real artist too.

Lizzy gave me a thumbs-up.

Ms. Silva asked Max to pass out an info sheet about the lirpaloof. Then she told us to read silently to ourselves.

After we were done reading about the lirpaloof, we talked more about birds and how they have

The lirpaloof

Description

Yellow throat. Bright red head with black feathers on top. Wings are black with white at the base.

Habitat

Open fields and scattered trees. Common perches are on fence posts. In shrubs, the lirpaloof makes nests of twigs, grass, and feathers.

Eggs

Lays 3–5 eggs that are bluish green. Both parents give food to nestlings. The young leave the nest about 2 weeks after hatching.

Diet

Fruit and insects, including bees, ants, beetles, and termites.

Sound

Short and flute-like.

hollow bones so they can fly. And they lay eggs, just like alligators.

Ms. Silva told us to color in the lirpaloof and to read over the sheet one more time.

"That way, by this afternoon," she said, "you'll be ready for your lirpaloof search."

"Will we get money from the newspaper if we take a picture?" asked Pablo.

"I don't think so," said Ms. Silva, "but I know you'll get a good feeling"—she patted her heart—"right here."

"I want a good cupcake feeling," said Mo. "Right here." Then he patted his stomach. A whole bunch of kids giggled. I felt a little jealous. Okay, a whole lot jealous. April Fools' Day was almost over, and I hadn't made any good pranks or gotten anyone to laugh. I needed some kind of magic binoculars that could help me see the best way to be funny.

Chapter Ten:

Best-Friend Talk

After lunch everyone spread out in the classroom for free-reading time.

I stomped over to the bookshelf, grabbed the first thing I saw, and flopped onto my desk chair.

Lizzy hurried over to me. "What's the matter, Ellie May?" she asked in a soft voice. "You look upset."

"Yeah, I've blown a gasket." That's what Nana tells Mom after she babysits my sisters at

her house in Los Angeles, and we fight the whole time. "What happened?" Lizzy's eyebrows lifted.

"I'm seriously mad I couldn't be funny."

"I think you're funny," whispered Lizzy. "Only you forgot to say 'April Fools' to Ava."

"Oh, right. I just thought she would know." Lizzy always remembers the important details. I shrugged. "Mo's funny. Ava is smart. You're artsy. I just want to be something too."

"But you are something," said Lizzy. "You make everyone around you notice the fun and exciting stuff. You never give up and—"

"Time to read, everyone," said Ms. Silva.

"Do you know that the center of the earth is made out of iron?" Pablo raised his thick book. "And in some places it's close to 9,000 degrees? I learned it from *Understanding Earthquake*s."

"Nice science facts, Pablo," said Ms. Silva.

"Hey, do you know what an earthquake's

favorite song is?" asked Mo. He wiggled in his beanbag chair and sang, "*Shake it off.*"

Everyone laughed. Even Ms. Silva.

Max, the copycat, shook so much that he almost fell out of his chair. The class laughed even harder.

Mo slapped Max a high-five.

And that's when I decided I wasn't giving up. April Fools' wasn't over yet.

Chapter Eleven

Mine Smells Funny

At last it was treat time.

"As you know, it was Ava's birthday this weekend," Ms. Silva said, standing in front of the sink. "So we're celebrating it today."

"And it's April Fools' Day," said Pablo.

Boy, did I know about that.

Ms. Silva carefully took down a tray of cupcakes from a shelf above the sink. She handed the tray to Ava.

Kids cheered. Ms. Silva smiled. Ava smiled. Everyone leaned forward in their seats to admire the cupcakes.

"They look professional," said Jamila.

"They're so beautiful you don't want to eat them," said Lizzy.

It was true. I eyed the cupcakes carefully. They were just what I needed to turn this April Fools' Day around. Pale peach icing covered the cupcakes in soft ripples. The green stems and pink roses topping the cupcakes looked almost real. A yellow-and-black-striped bumblebee buzzed over each flower.

Ms. Silva placed Ava's peach-colored napkins with silver dots on everyone's desks, and we sang "Happy Birthday."

"Ava, why don't you tell us a little bit about the cupcakes?" said Ms. Silva.

"I've been taking a baking class on Saturdays,"

Ava said. "I used buttercream icing." She slowed down her words and spoke loudly, like we were babies. "I used fondant to make the roses and the stems. Fondant, if you don't know, is icing that you can shape. It's like Play-Doh for chefs."

The class oohed and aahed at the fancy icing. Some clapped their hands. Sweetness filled the room.

"The air smells so good I want to eat it," said Pablo.

The compliments kept on coming as Ava handed out the cupcakes.

"You could sell these," said Max.

"You could frame them," exclaimed Jamila.

"They're made from zucchini, beets, and sauerkraut," said Ava. "It's a special recipe I learned from my baking teacher. The vegetables make the cupcakes extra moist, and they're good for you too." Some of the kids blinked in surprise.

I couldn't believe all that healthy stuff was mixed up together. It didn't make sense. A treat was supposed to be 100 percent sugar. Not vegetables. Ava and her horse Annabelle really did have a lot in common.

When Ava held out a cupcake for me, I studied it. How weird. It seemed normal even though it was filled with vegetables. Whatever it was filled with, it would help me with my latest plan.

"Mine smells funny," I said, which was a lie. I plugged my nose. "Pee-yew!"

A bunch of kids started to smell their cupcakes too.

"Mine smells awesome," said Mo.

I popped up from my desk. "You need to smell mine then." My plan was working perfectly so far.

Mo came closer to take a big sniff. That's when I pushed the cupcake right at his face! "April Fools!" I yelled, thinking Lizzy would be proud. But I got so excited for my surprise prank that I tripped a bit. The cupcake missed his sniffing nose and hit him right in the eye!

Mo shrieked. Lizzy gasped. Ava grunted, and Owen jumped out of his chair.

Everyone stared at the mashed-up cupcake all over Mo's face. Lizzy tried to whisper something to me, but I couldn't tell what it was.

"I definitely didn't see that coming," said Mo, rubbing icing off his eye. "I feel like a cupcake pirate. *Arghhh.*"

Ms. Silva hurried down the aisle. "Ellie May, I want you to sit down at your desk. You need to apologize."

"I'm really sorry," I said. "I didn't mean to get you in the eye."

"It's okay," said Mo, grinning. He licked his lips, and little puffs of icing floated to the ground like pieces of snow. "Smells good, tastes good, and looks good!"

Ms. Silva grabbed what was left of the smooshed cupcake and put it into the trash. "No birthday snack, Ellie May."

"But . . . but I was just trying to be—"

"In your seat. Now." Ms. Silva pointed to the clothespin with my name on it. My name was on the green good square. "It's going straight to the orange warning square. If it goes to red, there will be no recess on top of no snack. Which means no lirpaloof hunt!" She folded her arms. "What were you thinking, Ellie May?"

A bazillion eyes studied me. I could feel myself turning lava red.

"I was trying to be funny," I explained. "It's April Fools' Day. You're supposed to make people laugh." Kids stared. Some let out guffaws. That's a laugh that sounds like a mean snort.

Ms. Silva held up her hand. That meant she needed our attention. "One, two, three, eyes on me."

"One, two, eyes on you," the class chorused.

"It's fine to laugh *with* someone, but not *at* them," said Ms. Silva. "Just now you all were laughing at Ellie May for getting in trouble. And before that, Ellie May was trying to get you to laugh at Mo being attacked by a cupcake. Mo could've been hurt, and you were wasting Ava's generous treat, Ellie May."

I felt the slumpiest I'd ever felt. Ever.

"Everyone enjoys having fun," continued Ms. Silva, "but it's important to be funny in a way that makes everyone laugh—even the person you're pranking. For example, you could hand your friend an apple with a gummy worm stuck in it. That would be funny and tasty."

I felt fizzled and flat. And embarrassed. I guess I had just wanted to get attention. I sure didn't like it when my feelings got hurt. Even though Mo wasn't too upset and still got a new cupcake, I felt bad about getting so much cupcake all over him. I hung my head.

Ava quickly passed out the rest of the vegetable cupcakes. I sat silently and tried to avoid watching everyone.

Everyone ate them quickly. All you could hear

were lips smacking. And lots of frosting-filled mouths saying, “Yum.”

Behind me, Pablo wiped his mouth with the back of his hand. “That was the best cupcake I’ve ever had in my whole entire life.”

“Me too,” said Mo.

“Me three,” said Max.

Other kids like Owen and Jamila nodded in agreement.

Even Lizzy was nodding.

“The vanilla and chocolate flavors were all swirled together,” explained Pablo, “and the icing was so”—he rubbed his belly—“buttery. It was amazing. The best.”

The best cupcakes everyone ever had in their whole entire lives? My mouth watered. I tried not to remember that icing was my most favorite food. My shoulders went even slumpier. Nothing right now felt like April Fools’ Day fun.

"Ellie May, I wish I could have given you a bite," whispered Lizzy.

"It's okay. I wouldn't want you to get in trouble." I watched Lizzy pop her last piece into her mouth. The sweetness still hung in the air. And I wished I had some of it.

Thankfully Mo had been a good sport about it all. He could've made me feel a lot worse. I had to give it to him. He really is the funniest. Even with cake smashed all over his face. And I guess I hadn't thought about Ava's feelings before. She had gone to baking lessons and cooked for ten hundred years, and I had mashed up her treat. How could I make it up to her?

Chapter Twelve

Lirpaloof at Last!

"Who's ready for the lirpaloof search?" asked Ms. Silva. She wore a huge camera around her neck.

"Me!" chorused practically everyone. Only I wasn't so sure. Looking for a bird wasn't as good as a cupcake. And it would probably be boring. Plus I felt too embarrassed to be with my class right now. But the binoculars were pretty cool.

Ms. Silva had us grab our lirpaloof fact sheets and follow her outside.

As we stood on the blacktop, she counted us into groups of four. I was with Jamila, Max, and Lizzy.

"C'mon over here," said Ms. Silva, "and pick up a pair of binoculars to share with your group." She pointed to the bucket on the edge of the blacktop. "We're going to stay in our teams to officially search for the lirpaloof now."

The class hooted and clapped.

"You have to be very quiet. The lirpaloof easily frightens. So when you're looking, zip your lips. When you see it, quietly alert your classmates, and I'll make sure to take some photos."

My group headed to the back fence by the kickball field. We tiptoed to be extra quiet. I looked through the binoculars.

At first everything was all blurry. But then I focused. The low puffy clouds looked close enough to touch.

“I see something!” I couldn’t help but feel excited. “Something red!” I yelled.

“Shh,” said Jamila.

“Where?” asked Max.

I pointed to the fence post by the shed. “Over there.”

While I kept looking through the binoculars, the others raced to the fence. Jamila clip-clopped like a horse, and Max zigzagged. But Lizzy ran regularly. “Go, Lizzy!” I shouted.

“I actually won,” she cried. She’d gotten there first.

It was a red mitten.

"It's not even alive," Max grumbled. He threw it to me.

"Wait a minute," I said. "My mom will be super happy." It was my lost mitten that my grandma from Philadelphia had sent me. She didn't understand that nobody in Orange County wears mittens to school, because it's not cold like it is where Grandma lives. But still, I'd brought them in for morning sharing ages ago. "I've been looking for it for a hundred million years!"

"If it was a hundred million years ago," Ava said, "then it would be from a cave person. This is about science, Ellie May. You're supposed to be looking for the lirpaloof. Honestly."

But I didn't care, because I was seeing something cool with the binoculars. Something tiny and shiny and yellow.

It wasn't a bird.

I jumped up and down. I waved. "Look!" I pointed down at my feet.

A bunch of kids came running over, including Lizzy. "Wow," she said. "A whole patch of buttercups."

"You can make a huge chain with them," I said. "Longer than your whole body. It would be big enough for"—I squeezed my eyes to think better—"an elephant necklace."

Lizzy gave me a huge smile.

"Here," I said, plucking a buttercup and handing it to Ava. "If it shines on your chin, it means you like butter."

She put it under her chin.

For a moment I tried to think of a buttercup and horse joke. But I stopped myself. "I'm blinking in all the brightness shining under your chin," I said, shielding my eyes. "Wow-ee, you do like butter. That's why you're such a good cupcake maker."

"Thanks, Ellie May," said Ava.

"Yeah, well, sorry I called them stinky," I told her. "'Cause they weren't. They smelled like vanilla creamy deliciousness. I guess I wasn't so funny earlier."

"Well, you're always fun."

I liked that. It was nice of her to say. Maybe I wasn't always funny, but I was fun.

"Hey, want to hear me whinny?"

"Sure," she said.

I tossed my mane and made horse sounds.

"Perfect," said Ava.

"I promise I don't have any more vegetable pranks. If you have one, lettuce know," I joked.

"You don't even have *one* more?" asked Ava.

"Vegetable jokes?" I shrugged. "Beets me." Everyone around me laughed. I looked up and laughed too. The sky was so blue and crisp, I could drink it.

And best of all, we kept on finding stuff.

Owen found an empty bird's nest.

Ava found a poofy dandelion and made a birthday wish.

Jamila spotted a bird with a red head that we thought was the lirpaloof. Only Ms. Silva told us it was a western tanager.

We searched every bush.

The breeze blew like it was trying to gently blow out a happy-birthday candle for the world. We stared at the fence posts until our eyes hurt.

We stared into the cottony white clouds. Only it's hard to tell what birds really look like when they're flying way up high. They're just little *v*'s.

Through the binoculars, we saw tree bark up close, airplanes in the sky, and the buttons on someone's shirt.

Finally Ms. Silva motioned us over to her. She stood under the basketball net. "If we want to attract the lirpaloof, we should try its call." Tipping back her head, she went, "Coo coo eep, coo coo eep." She turned to look at us. "Now you try it."

Everyone tipped back their heads up to the clouds and made the lirpaloof call.

"Coo coo eep!" I called along with everyone else. "Coo coo eep!" We sounded like an entire flock of lirpaloofs. A mommy, daddy, and a whole bunch of kid lirpaloofs!

Only they didn't call back to us.

As much as we tried, the only thing we heard was ourselves.

Ms. Silva clapped her hands. "Everyone, come quickly," she said. "There's been a very important discovery!" She pointed to the part of the blacktop farthest from the school.

My heart went all thumpy. We rushed over. Right at the corner was a giant bucket of sidewalk chalk in every color.

"Class," said Ms. Silva, her voice urgent. "Quickly. Grab a piece of chalk."

I got a baby-blue piece. Lizzy got a whole purple one. That made me happy. Purple is her first-favorite color. Tied with aquamarine.

"Okay, in a few seconds you're going to understand all there is to know about the rare lirpaloof," said Ms. Silva.

Funnily enough, I was really into this whole bird search. "I'm so excited, my heart wants to come out of my chest," I said.

"Mine, too," said Mo. "It wants to fly away like a bird."

We all giggled. In an I'm-laughing-*with*-you kind of way. The best kind of way.

"Okay, I want each one of you to write out *lirpaloof* on the blacktop," said Ms. Silva. "Today, the blacktop is our giant chalkboard."

Everyone did. I tried to write as straight and

neat as Ms. Silva does on the board. But not like when she writes in cursive. I don't know how to make my letters swirly and important yet.

"Okay, now I want you to write out *lirpaloof* backward," said Ms. Silva.

"Backward?" Ava asked, her voice rising in surprise.

"Yes," said Ms. Silva

"Hey, mine says 'fool April'!" I said, blinking in surprise.

"So does mine," said Mo.

"Mine too," said Lizzy.

"And mine." Ava studied her letters. "I don't get it."

"April Fools!" said Ms. Silva. "*Lirpaloof* is 'April fool' backward." A huge smile stretched across her face. "The lirpaloof is a fake bird."

"Oh. *Oh*! I get it now!" I laughed really hard.

"Me too!" Ava covered her mouth as she giggled.

foolapril

"Ms. Silva," said Pablo, laughing. "You got us *really* good."

"I think so," she said, taking photos. Kids kept pointing at the letters on the blacktop. Some spelled it out for themselves with a piece of chalk.

Mo gripped his forehead. "My mind is so blown, my brain might explode."

"I truly believed the lirpaloof was real," I gushed. "That was the best April Fools' prank ever!" I'm guessing this is what my mom would call clever.

Everyone was laughing. And nobody was laughing *at* anyone, so I knew it was the good kind of joke.

"Happy April Fools' Day, everyone," Ms. Silva said.

And it was. Happy, I mean. And not boring. And fun.

It was also tasty. That's because after school,

on the bus, Ava gave me a leftover cupcake. "I had an extra one," she said. "I thought you might want to try my birthday snack."

My stomach did happy somersaults. "Thanks," I said, biting into a part with green icing. A whole lot of sweet buttery goodness melted in my mouth.

Chapter Thirteen
Hard Day/Good Day

"So how was school?" asked Mom. She was cutting up little red potatoes for dinner. I was scratching Diesel under his chin. "Did Ava enjoy her birthday snacks?"

"Oh yes," I said. "She loves vegetables. She likes vegetables so much she put them in her cupcakes. Like zucchini. I thought it was a crazy idea. But it wasn't. It tasted so good."

I told her all about the super good lirpaloof joke. Then I took a deep breath and explained all about the cupcake incident. I spoke fast so I could get all the bad parts out of the way. How I had tried so hard to get a big laugh on April Fools' Day, only I had messed up. How my clothespin had gone on the not-good orange square. She listened really hard. When she sat me down on the couch, she didn't say she wanted to call my teacher. Or hold a family conference.

"It sounds like it ended up being a good day," she said, "even if parts of it were hard. We all have hard days now and then."

"Even you?" I asked.

"Even me," she said.

My throat felt a little squeezey as I remembered the sweet smell of the icing filling up the classroom. And how I didn't get to eat my cupcake with the other kids.

"Remember that carrot cake at Aunt Leslie's wedding? I think I'd like to try it again," I admitted. "Maybe you can find the recipe."

Mom smiled. "We can arrange that."

"And you won't be too busy with your work, saving the ocean?"

"No," she said, smiling. "I won't be."

"What?" asked Midge. She raced in from the family room.

"We're going to taste some carrot cake," said Mom. "We'll plan a baking weekend."

"I can't wait, because you're good at finding recipes on the Internet." I nodded over at her laptop. "Bet you'll find the best cake ever."

"Did someone say cake?" asked Dad, entering the room with Lexie. Diesel wagged his tail.

"Yes, but at this point, it's just a plan." Mom wrote a note to herself in her phone, then turned it off and put it away on the shelf.

“I like cake plans,” said Dad.

“Hey, we did something really cool at school,” I said. “Ms. Silva took us outside to go bird watching.”

“We never did that when I was in second grade,” said Lexie.

“We looked through binoculars and saw lots of stuff,” I said.

“Did you see outer space?” asked Midge.

“No, you need a telescope for that,” explained Dad. “Binoculars are different.”

“They are for viewing things at a closer distance,” said Mom.

“Yeah, we saw a nest in a tree.” I raised my hand to put up to the ceiling. “And airplanes in the sky and”—I pulled the red mitten from my pocket—“this!”

Mom clapped her hands. “Wow. I never thought we’d find your mitten.”

"It's a wonder what you can find with binoculars," said Dad, peering outside.

"Do we have binoculars, Dad?" I asked.

"We do," Dad said.

"I could take you guys out in the backyard," I said, "to look for a really cool bird."

"Yes! Yes!" shouted Midge.

"That sounds like a good idea, honey," said Mom.

"There have been some hummingbirds where the snapdragon bush is blooming," said Dad. "I'll be right back."

"Sounds kind of boring," said Lexie.

"But I'm really good at making things fun," I said. "You'll see."

"I guess I can go for a little bit," said Lexie. Diesel's tail swished super fast. He wanted to go outside too.

Dad reappeared with a pair of binoculars.

"Ready?" I asked.

Dad put the binoculars around his neck. Lexie helped pull on Midge's boots, and Mom gave me a thumbs-up.

I put my fingers to my lips. "In order to see this rare bird, we'll have to be very quiet and very still."

Midge shouted, "I can be quiet!"

"Shh," said Lexie. "Quiet means whispering."

"What bird are we going to find, Ellie May?" whispered Midge.

"The lirpaloof," I whispered back, winking at Mom. Then we all linked arms and headed for the backyard.

April Fools' Day History and Traditions

The origin of April Fools' Day is a bit of a mystery. Some claim that the holiday grew out of ancient festivals that celebrated the end of winter. Many point to the Roman festival of Hilaria in late March. During this merry festival, people enjoyed wearing disguises. Others consider the medieval Feast of Fools—when masters waited on servants and appointed a Lord of Misrule to oversee the rowdy celebration—as the true origin of April Fools' Day.

One legend even claims that the tradition of April Fools' was actually started during the thirteenth century by the English town of Gotham, when the townspeople tricked King

John from taking their land. They had heard he wanted to build a hunting lodge in Gotham. When the king's soldiers burst into the town, they found everyone acting crazy, and doing things like trying to drown fish. The king decided to hunt elsewhere since Gotham was obviously a town full of fools.

While we might not know the true origin of the holiday, countries all around the world celebrate lighthearted spring holidays. In India there's Holi, also known as the Festival of Colors, when people laugh and celebrate spring by throwing colored powder. In Scotland they prank one another on Hunt the Gowk Day. *Gowk* is another word for a cuckoo—a bird that makes a silly-sounding call. In France, April Fools' Day is called Poisson d'Avril, which means April Fish. On that day, jokers tape a paper fish to unsuspecting people's backs.

Throughout the years there have been some rather successful April Fools' pranks. A most famous one occurred in 1957, when a BBC news program declared that the Swiss were enjoying an unusually large spaghetti crop. The program showed images of farmers harvesting spaghetti from trees. Huge numbers of viewers called in wanting to know how they could purchase a spaghetti tree!

On April Fools' Day many schools enjoy a day of good fun, where everyone is in on the joke. Some classrooms enjoy Backward Day, where children wear clothing backward and even inside-out. Some teachers hold contests where students recite their alphabet backward or sing songs like "Row, Row, Row Your Boat" backward. Many families enjoy harmless April Fools' pranks such as filling juice glasses with Jell-O. What are some of your favorite April Fools' Day traditions?